TICK-TOCK TICK-TOCK

BLUE PLANET

GONZAGUE DUFOUR

ILLUSTRATIONS BY JEAN NESTARES

Copyright © 2015 by Gonzague Dufour. 707048
Library of Congress Control Number: 2015903199

ISBN: Softcover   978-1-5035-4823-7
        Hardcover   978-1-5035-4822-0
        EBook   978-1-5035-4824-4

Print information available on the last page

Rev. date: 06/30/2015

To order additional copies of this book, contact:
Xlibris
1-888-795-4274
www.Xlibris.com
Orders@Xlibris.com

To all the children in the world:
"LET'S DO SOMETHING!"
Thank you
to Jacky for her love and support
to Jean for the beautiful illustrations
to Eunice, Hannah and Jim

1

My iceberg is melting
My forest is devastated
My ocean is polluted
My savannah is ravaged

We are 4 friends living in different places on earth speaking to each other online. Sikut the polar bear, Blau the dolphin, M'Ba the elephant and Jim the wild boar.

My name is Sikut and I am a young polar bear, I live on an iceberg. My iceberg is a big piece of ice, a gigantically huge piece of ice, even larger than a football field. What is really amazing, is that my iceberg is floating and moving on the ocean with water everywhere. I love to bowl with ice balls on my iceberg with my friends.

4

The problem is that my iceberg is melting. Last year, it was not really visible. But this year, I am almost certain that my "football field" is smaller. To check, I spoke to my grandpa and asked him. My grandpa is an old, wise polar bear. He has lived here for many, many years and he knows absolutely everything.

"Grandpa, do you think that my iceberg is melting?"

"Sikut, I am not sure, but I think you may be right. I have never seen this before, but all around us, everything is changing. The ice is melting and disappearing faster and faster."

"This is horrible! My iceberg may disappear and then where would I go?"

"It may be just here, but why don't you speak to one of your friends, for example, Blau, the young dolphin?"

Sikut takes his white cell phone and calls Blau.
"Blau, there is a real problem here. My iceberg is melting. We don't know why. Do you have any problems in the ocean?"

Blau lives in the Pacific Ocean, where he can swim in the deep, blue water with huge waves, a lot of great food, and many special friends. He spends his day jumping out of the water, racing with his friends, and sometimes getting next to boats crossing the huge ocean.

"Sikut, it is bad, really bad. Here, we have another problem. The other day I was jumping as high as I could out of the water - it's so nice to make those big splashes - and I saw something really strange.

I thought it was an island, a big island, but there were no trees, no mountains, no flowers, no birds. As I got closer, I found out that it was plastic bottles, thousands and thousands of plastic bottles, together with plastic bags and pieces of wood. It was all just trash. Before, it was water, lovely blue clear water. Now it is garbage."

As you did, I went to my grandpa, an old and very wise dolphin, and asked him: "Grandpa, what's going on? Did you see that big, floating mountain of garbage?" "Yes, Blau, people call it the 6th Continent. It's big, very big and growing. Millions of empty bottles "THEY" are throwing away."

"Icebergs are melting, a continent of empty bottles is building up... What's going on?"
I should speak to M'Ba.
Blau takes his blue phone and calls M'Ba, his friend, the young elephant.
"M'ba, I have a problem. I just discovered a new continent full of garbage and it's killing
the fish and everything else around it. Do you have a similar problem where you live? "

M'ba is a young female elephant. She lives in Ambreli Africa, a beautiful place, where many wild animals run free and are protected from people who want to hunt them. It is called the savannah.

"We too have a problem. The other day, while exploring the savannah with my family, we were looking for good, green tree leaves. Usually, in that place we see a big elephant, who is a little bit old and solitary, yet nice and funny. Guess what? Today, he was not there!"

My grandma said: "M'ba, you should know that some very bad people are killing our friends just to take their tusks and sell the ivory to other bad people. It is illegal, but many of our friends are being killed every year in Africa."

A 6th continent, the iceberg is melting and here they are hunting elephants for ivory, what on earth is going on?

M'ba takes her black cell phone and calls Jim the young, wild boar.

"Jim, I have a problem. Something really bad is happening. Sikut's iceberg is melting. Blau has discovered a 6th continent - "a trash continent"- and here in Africa, they are killing my friends for their ivory. Do you have the same problem in Europe?"

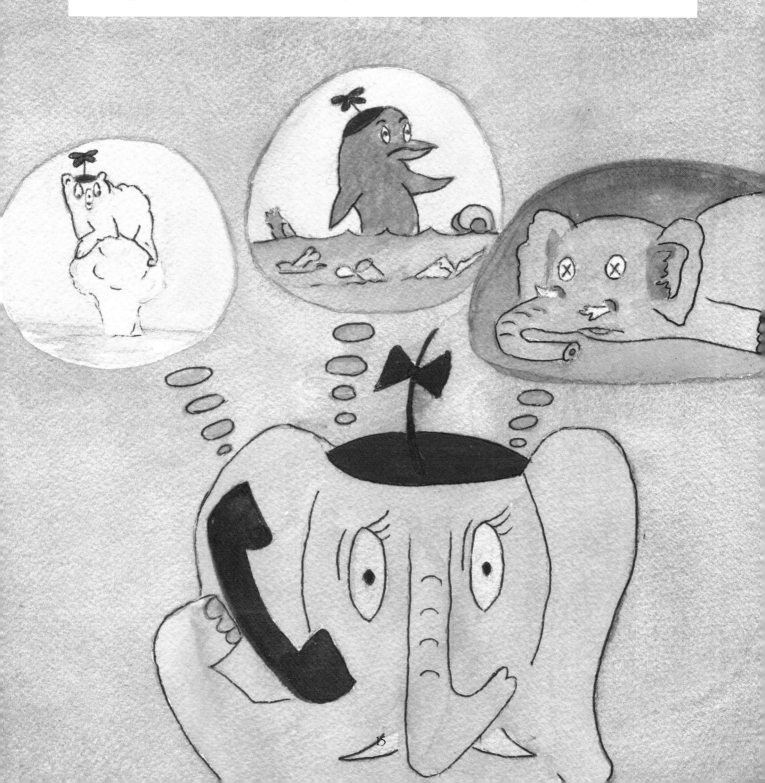

Jim lives in a beautiful wooded area. It's a large forest where a lot of animals, such as deer, rabbits, foxes, wild boars, squirrels and birds can live, protected and move around freely.

Jim spends his time looking for acorns, potatoes, and farmers' apples.
But the other day, he saw a very big and noisy yellow "animal" in his forest.

He ran as fast as he could to see his grandpa, a large and wise wild boar with sharp tusks:

"Grandpa, what is this big scary yellow animal I saw in the forest this morning? "

"It's called a bulldozer. Humans use it to destroy things like the forest, faster and faster."

"But why here, why in this forest?"

"These people have decided to build a golf course and to build hundreds of nice houses around it."

"But why grandpa? The forest is beautiful. Many animals have their home there and will die if they do it."

Jim decides to call his friends.
"Hello my friends! We have a big problem, it is the same everywhere!
The ice is melting!!
Trees are being taken down!!
The ocean is polluted and animals are being killed!!
I don't know what we can do! I guess we animals are defenseless, right?
I am so upset!
You know what? I am going to speak with my friend Tom. He is a young boy, who loves our forests and its animals. I wonder if he knows anything about it?"

Tom lives in the forest with his family. His dad is a forest warden, and he knows every corner of the forest.

They meet far from the bulldozer, in one of the small clearings.

Tom had brought juicy apples and when Jim had finished eating he said:

"Tom, have you heard about

The iceberg melting

The 6th continent

The hunt for ivory

and the destruction of the forests?"

"Yes, I have. We spoke about it in class the other day and THAT IS NOT ALL! Everywhere it's the same: flooding, storms, huge fires, oceans polluted, rare species disappearing, droughts, glaciers melting....
My father told me that we CAN do something to change this, but I don't know what!"

"Let's call Sikut, Blau, M'Ba and their friends. I am sure they will have an idea."
Indeed, as Jim met with Tom, M'ba, Blau and Sikut met with other young people
and after many days they became true friends: Mussa, the Massai warrior,
Akamu, the Hawaian and Ahnah, the Inuk.

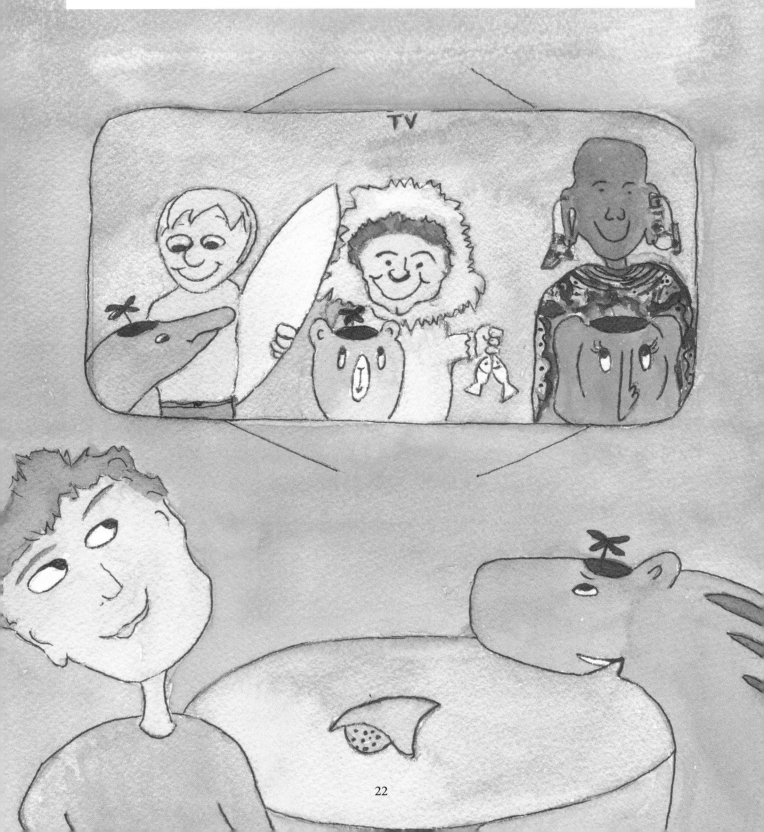

They all agreed that this is serious and urgent.

They don't want to disappear under millions of plastic bottles, be killed by poachers, lose their icebergs, or see their forests razed and disappear.

Together we want to make this VISIBLE !!

Jim and Tom with their friends, both human and animal, organized a big march.

All the animals of the forest came to face the bulldozers, and Tom gathered his schoolmates and sent messages and pictures everywhere.

Since then, the project has been stopped and the forest has been saved.

Sikut and Ahnah (wise woman in Inuk) decided to paint their iceberg with a big red sign right down the middle: SOI "Save Our Iceberg". They made sure that a picture and a video would be posted online. Since then, people from all over the world have been working to find the best ways to stop the melting of the icebergs.

M'ba and Mussa organized a surveillance party. M'ba and her family would inform Mussa as soon as they saw a poacher. Mussa then would warn the guards in the Ambreli National Park. The poachers would be arrested and put in jail. Since then, no more elephants have been killed in Ambreli Park.

Blau and Akamu, with thousands of big and small fish and with the help of fishermen, would push the 6th continent in front of nice beaches.
Then surely, people would react.

Since then, elephants don't disappear in Ambreli, there are no more golf courses or houses in the forest, the 6th continent is nearly gone and the icebergs do not melt anymore.

Their plans have worked BUT YOU...
What can you do to protect your planet?

A beautiful blue planet...Earth.

Four friends living in the North Pole, in Africa, in the Ocean, and in a forest.

Four friends discovering that the planet is in danger.

Four friends deciding to do something to protect their iceberg, forest, savannah and the elephants.

And you, what can you do to protect this beautiful Planet?

CPSIA information can be obtained at www.ICGtesting.com
Printed in the USA
BVIW12n0013040815
411406BV00002B/3